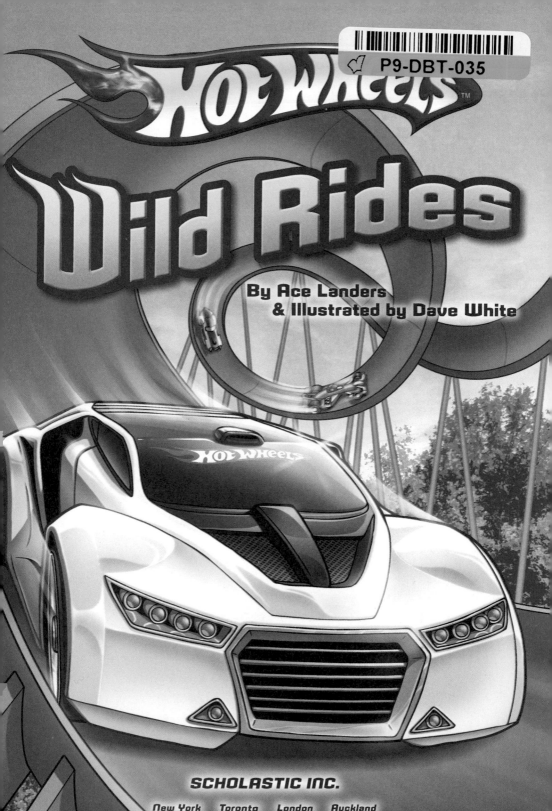

HOT WHEELS™

Wild Rides

By Ace Landers
& Illustrated by Dave White

SCHOLASTIC INC.

New York   Toronto   London   Auckland

Sydney   Mexico City   New Delhi   Hong Kong

ISBN-10: 0-545-15347-6   ISBN-13: 978-0-545-15347-8

12 11 10 9 8 7 6 5 4 3   9 10 11 12 13/0

Printed in the U.S.A.   40
First printing, November 2009

Welcome to the mystery race.

None of the racers
know what to expect.

First, the cars race downhill.

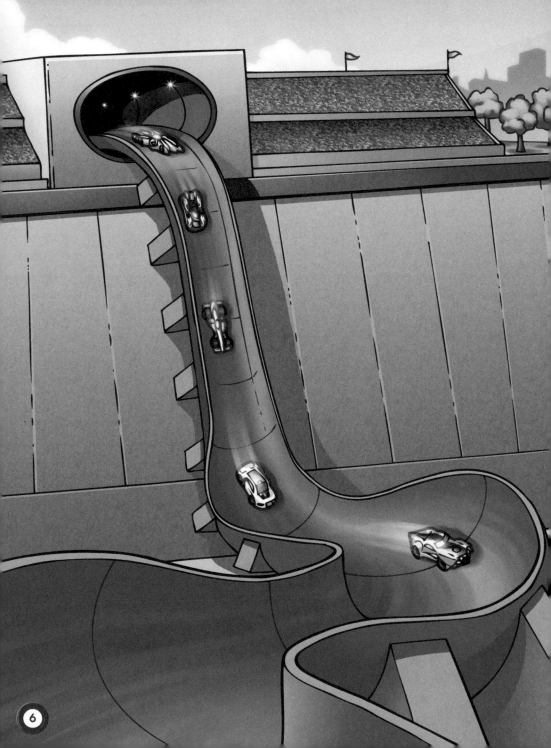

The walls are steep.

An ice rink is at the bottom of the track!

The cars skid.

The white and red cars take one tunnel.

The yellow and blue cars take the other.

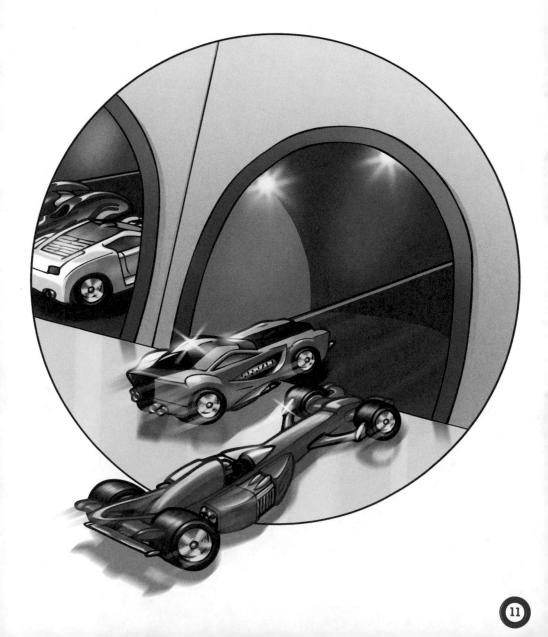

Watch out for deep holes!

The white car takes the ramp.
The red car weaves around the holes.

The red car almost gets stuck.

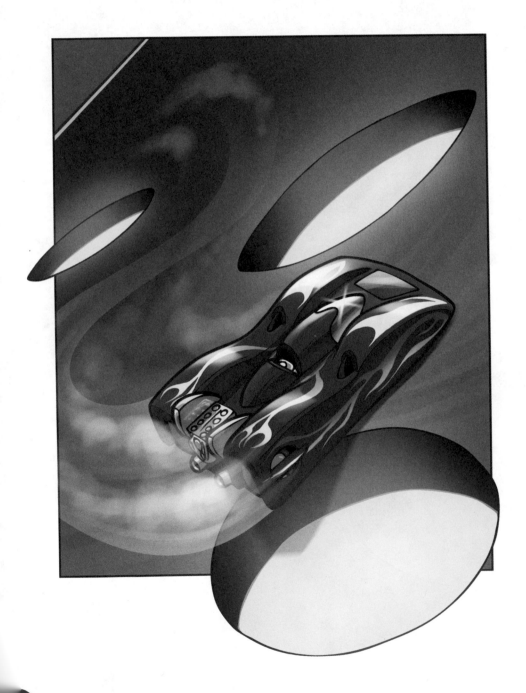

The white car lands the jump!

In the other tunnel, the cars need to look out. *Swoosh!*

The blue car gets hit!

It spins out.
But the blue car is still in the race!

All the cars race to the
end of the tunnels.

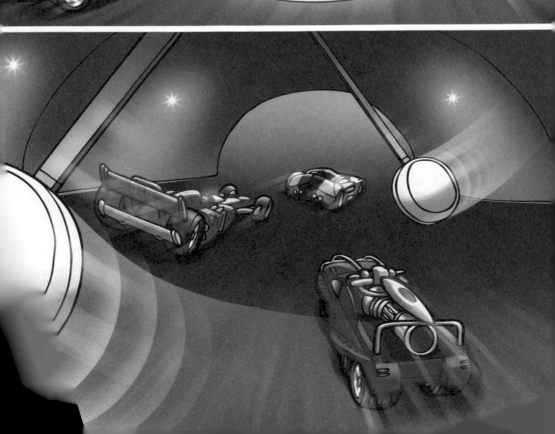

The racecars are all back on the same track!

There are three tunnels ahead.
Which tunnel will each car choose?

The white car's tunnel
leads to a big ramp!

The red car's tunnel leads to a bridge.

The bridge falls down while the red car drives across it!

The blue car tries to drive across.
But the bridge is gone!

The yellow car's tunnel leads to a sharp turn!

Then it hits a catapult and sails through the air!

Which car will win?

The yellow car crosses
the finish line first!